PRINCESS NATASHA

student · secret agent · princess

™

#3 Game Over

Text by Stephanie Peters

Created by Larry Schwarz

Visit Princess Natasha every day at
www.princessnatasha.com.

Watch Princess Natasha on CARTOON NETWORK™
and anytime online on the KOL™ service at
KW: Princess Natasha.

LITTLE, BROWN & COMPANY
LB kids™
NEW YORK BOSTON LONDON
www.lb-kids.com

Little, Brown and Company
1271 Avenue of the Americas, New York, NY 10020
Visit our Web site at www.lb-kids.com

LB kids is an imprint of Little, Brown and Company Books for Young Readers.
The logo design and name, LB kids, are trademarks.

First Edition: August 2006

Based on the KOL™ cartoon created by Animation Collective, Inc.

Library of Congress Cataloging-in-Publication Data

Peters, Stephanie True, 1965-
  Game over / text by Stephanie Peters ; [illustrations by Animation Collective].—1st ed.
      p. cm.— (Princess Natasha ; #3)
  "Based on the series created by Larry Schwarz."
  "Based on the KOL cartoon created by Animation Collective."
  ISBN 0-316-15506-3 (trade pbk.)
  I. Schwarz, Laurence. II. Animation Collective. III. Title. IV. Series: Peters, Stephanie True. Princess Natasha ; #3.
PZ7.P441833Gam 2006
[Fic]—dc22
                                        2005022788

10 9 8 7 6 5 4 3 2 1

COM-MO

Printed in the United States of America

A Brief Zoravian History

Deep in the Carpathian Mountains lies the ancient kingdom of Zoravia. Usually, the people of this country live in peace and harmony. But there are times when darkness falls across this fair land—a darkness known as Lubek.

Fifteen years earlier, Lubek inherited control of Zoravia. But the people had long despised Lubek. They voted him off the throne and elected his brother, Carl, in his place.

Lubek fled to America and began scheming against his former homeland. For years, his exact whereabouts remained a mystery. Then Zoravian Intelligence discovered his secret identity. By day, Lubek works as a high school principal and science teacher in a small town in Illinois called . . . Zoravia.

Once known as Fountain Park, the town changed its name in honor of King Carl, Queen Lena, and their fourteen-year-old daughter, Princess Natasha. Natasha had never met her evil uncle, but she had spent her life preparing to defeat him.

And now, she'll have her chance. Trained as a secret agent, Natasha has come to Illinois, where she poses as an exchange student at Fountain Park High. No one—not her host family, her friend Maya, or her fellow students—can ever know her true identity. If Lubek ever found out who she was, it would be the end of Natasha—and her beloved Zoravia.

Chapter One

Flower Power

Brrzap! Blam! Blam! Zing! Wackawackawacka-wacka!

"Is that a new language, KC?"

Natasha—princess of Zoravia, foreign exchange student, and undercover secret agent—leaned against her bedroom door and stared at the boy playing a game on her computer. KC O'Brien, the younger son in Natasha's American host family, kept his eyes glued to the screen.

Natasha stepped into the room. "I know a kid who forgot to blink when he played video games. Know what happened to him?"

KC grunted and continued to attack the keyboard with his fingers.

"His eyes got so dried out they cracked."

That got KC's attention. "Really?" he said, turning to look at her with great interest.

"Yep." She pulled up a chair and sat next to him. "He can still see, but he told me it's like looking through a broken window."

KC seemed to consider what she'd said.

"That didn't really happen, did it?" he finally asked.

Natasha raised an eyebrow.

"Yeah, you made it up," KC said more confidently.

"Then why are you suddenly blinking so much?"

KC stopped blinking.

Natasha nodded at the screen. "What are you playing, anyway?"

"It's a new game I downloaded from the high school Web site. All the kids are playing it."

"Uh-huh. Next question: Why are you playing it on my computer?"

"Mom's lookin' up stuff on hers."

"What about—"

"Greg's IMing Kelly on his." Greg was KC's handsome older brother. Kelly was Greg's irritating girlfriend.

"But don't you have a—"

KC jerked a thumb over his shoulder. "My handheld isn't working." The small computer was on her floor in a puddle of water.

"How'd it get so wet?" she asked.

"Fell in the toilet."

Natasha grimaced. "Before or after you used it?"

"The handheld or the toilet?"

"Never mind." She left to get a towel from the bathroom. When she got back, KC had returned to his game. Natasha cleaned up the puddle—praying that it was just plain toilet water.

"Listen, KC," she said, "I really need to use my computer now."

"Just let me get past this level," KC answered, his fingers moving furiously over the keys.

Natasha pulled a textbook from her backpack. "Come on, KC, finish up!" she said impatiently.

"What's the rush?"

Natasha started flipping through the textbook. "I've got a ton of science homework for Mr. Lubek's class and—"

"I love Mr. Lubek."

Natasha paused in mid-flip. "Come again?"

"Mr. Lubek is the best."

Natasha's jaw dropped in astonishment. To the best of her knowledge, KC—and just about everyone else she knew—despised Lubek. "KC, are—are you all right?"

 KC blinked. His fingers started tapping the keys again. "Almost done with this level," he replied. "One more *brrzap* and a *wackawacka- wackawacka* and . . . there!" He clicked his way out of the game and stood up.

Natasha looked at him searchingly.

"Uh, what's up?" KC said.

Natasha looked away. "Nothing, I guess."

But deep inside, instinct told her something— something *bad*—was most definitely up.

Chapter Two

An Alarming Alert

Natasha kept a close eye on KC the rest of the night and the next morning. To her relief, his behavior seemed perfectly normal—or as normal as KC's behavior ever was.

He probably just said those things to bug me, she thought on the way to school.

But if that were true, then her best friend was out to bug her, too.

"Man," she said to Maya when they met at their lockers, "I couldn't believe how much

7

homework Lubek—"

Maya cut her off. "Mr. Lubek is the best teacher I have ever had!" she gushed.

Greg joined them. "You talking about my favorite principal?"

Maya nodded enthusiastically. "He's the

man who puts the 'pal' in 'principal'!"

"I'm going to ask him if I can help out in the classroom!"

"Not if I ask him first!" They slammed their lockers shut and raced each other down the hallway.

Natasha stared after them in disbelief. Then she pinched her arm. *Okay, that hurt. So that means this isn't some nightmare I can wake up from!*

The nightmare continued throughout the morning. Students everywhere were singing the praises of Mr. Lubek. By lunchtime, her head was spinning.

"You've got an alert!"

Natasha was in the cafeteria line when she heard the voice coming from her backpack. It was her Booferberry, the small telecommunicator that was her primary link to her parents. When it went off, it meant that her father was calling—and *that* meant Lubek, archenemy of Zoravia, was up to no good again.

"You've got an alert!"

The boy in front of her turned. "Yo. Didja say somethin'?"

"Me? Nope!" She pretended to hunt in her

backpack for her lunch money. "Where did I stash that cash?" She found her Booferberry and hit the mute button. "Oh, rats," she said, shouldering her pack again, "I must have left my money in my coat pocket. Guess I'll just have to get out of line."

The boy looked at her like he couldn't care less what she did.

Natasha left the cafeteria and hurried to the

nearest bathroom. It was a single seater with a door that locked, perfect for listening to secret messages.

When she was safely locked inside, she yanked her Booferberry from her backpack and looked at the screen.

"Dad?"

Her father's handsome face materialized on

the screen. "Hello, Natasha. Are you well?"

"Same as always. What's going on?"

"Lubek is what's going on," King Carl answered solemnly.  "We don't know his exact plan but believe that it involves brainwashing the children of Zoravia into believing that he is a good man, a natural leader, and—"

Someone pounded on the bathroom door and jiggled the knob.

"Excuse me?" an angry female voice called. "Whoever you are, you are in *my* stall!"

Natasha groaned. She'd recognize that voice anywhere. It was Kelly. Kelly was pretty—pretty to look at, but also pretty dumb, pretty bossy, and right now, pretty annoyed that someone had dared to use "her" stall.

"Dad, I'd better go," Natasha whispered. "But I'll tell you this: I think Lubek's testing his brainwashing technique on the kids here first! You would not believe the things I've been hearing them say today! I'll be in touch when I find out what's happening."

She signed off and put away her Booferberry. To make her visit to the bathroom seem legit, she flushed the toilet and washed her hands.

"Finally!" Kelly pushed past Natasha when the door opened.

"Didn't realize it was an emergency," Natasha said. "Well, I hope everything comes out all right!"

Chapter Three

Down and Out

Late that night, when she thought everyone was asleep, Natasha put a call through to her Zoravian spy partner, Oleg Boynski. She hoped they'd be able to get to the bottom of Lubek's plan together. Oleg usually answered his cell phone on the first ring. But tonight Natasha let it ring six times before she gave up.

Looks like I'm on my own. She changed into her spy suit and tiptoed to her window, ready to escape into the darkness. Then she saw a strange light flashing in the backyard below and heard voices. She pulled back and listened.

"KC, you flea-infested, maggot-ridden hair ball," Greg called angrily, "I'm going to get you if it takes me all night!"

"If I'm a flea-infested, maggot-ridden hair ball," KC taunted from another part of the yard, "why do you want me so bad?"

Wonder what KC did to Greg this time? Natasha thought. KC was a menace—and also a champion hider. She knew it could take a while for Greg to find his brother. So leaving through the window was out.

She crossed her room and pressed her ear to her door. Mr. and Mrs. O'Brien were talking in the hallway.

Doesn't anyone in this family go to bed at a

decent hour?

She waited until the O'Briens had gone into their bedroom and then slipped into the hallway. As quietly  as she could, she sneaked down the stairs to the first floor and peeked out the family-room window. Greg was still searching the backyard for his little brother.

Rats! How am I gonna get out of here? Her gaze fell on a laundry basket overflowing with dirty clothes. It sat near the door to the basement, where the washer and dryer were. And the basement had a separate door to the yard.

Perfect! she thought. *I can escape through the basement. And I'll use the laundry as my cover for being down there!*

She opened the door at the top of the basement stairs and reached in to flick on the light.

Nothing happened.

Bulb must be burned out, she figured. She peered down into the darkness and then, with a sigh, picked up the laundry basket.

"*Umph!*"

The load was heavier than it looked.

There better not be anything in my way!

She stepped down. Instead of a flat stair, her foot landed on something round.

"*Whoooaaaaa!*" The rest of the trip to the basement took two seconds flat.

"*Oomph!*" She landed headfirst in the pile of dirty laundry. When she sat up, one of Greg's smelly, sweat-stained T-shirts was wrapped around her head.

"Ew, ew, *ew!*"

She threw aside the shirt, climbed over the

rest of the laundry and ran to the basement door. She opened it a crack and peered out. The yard was empty. Staying low, she tiptoed across the lawn to the garage and took cover behind some garbage cans.

A hand grabbed her wrist.

Instinct and years of martial arts training took over. Natasha twisted her arm up and out, forcing the hand to break its grip. Then she connected a solid

roundhouse kick to her assailant's body. She was primed to strike with a hook-jab combo when her attacker gasped her name.

"Natasha, wait!"

She dropped her fists. "Oleg?"

Her spy partner emerged from the dark, dusting her footprint off the front of his white lab coat.

"Why didn't you tell me it was you?" Natasha demanded.

"I was in mid-swallow," Oleg explained. "Have you ever tried talking while swallowing? It's physically impossible. Like keeping your eyes open when you sneeze. Or laughing without smiling."

Natasha eyed the open garbage can. "Um, what exactly were you eating?"

He held up a thin brown rod. "Zoravian yak jerky. Want some?"

Natasha made a face. "I'll pass. What—besides snacking on cured meat products—are you doing here?"

"I received a message from King Carl to shadow Lubek. I tracked him to the waterfront

area, but then I lost him. I think we can find him on your Locator. You do have it with you, don't you?"

Natasha pulled her Lubek Locator from her utility belt. When given Lubek's general location, the small computer could usually pinpoint her uncle's exact whereabouts. She entered the coordinates for the waterfront. The Locator scanned the area and gave a beep.

She frowned. "It says he's in the middle of the lake!"

Oleg checked the screen. "No, there's an island there."

"An island?" Natasha echoed. "Hmmm . . . We better take the copter then. Come on!"

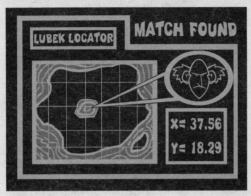

Chapter Four

Up and Down

Ten minutes later, Natasha and Oleg were wing-
ing above the lake in the helicopter. The night
sky was ink black and the lake was no brighter.
Luckily, Natasha had her super-powered, high-
tech, and unbelievably stylish glasses with
her. She set them to night vision and searched
the waves.

"I see the island!" she called.

Suddenly the copter was caught in a search-
light. "I think Lubek's onto us," Oleg cried. "I'll

use evasive maneuvers. You get on your air-board and get going!"

Natasha strapped her board to her feet and opened the helicopter door. She waited until they were directly over the island and then yelled, "I'm outta here!"

She pushed off and dropped into the night sky. Oleg swung the copter up and away from her. The search-light stayed with him.

Arms out, Natasha surfed the wind,

slaloming on the currents to keep from falling too quickly. Even so, the island raced up toward her. Treetops loomed into view.

Ouch! No thank you!

She swung the board's nose in a new direction. A rocky outcrop appeared beneath her.

Next!

She was losing altitude fast when she saw a sandy strip of land.

Ladies and gentlemen, we have a winner!

She did a quarter-turn backflip to avoid a tree branch and aimed for the beachfront. A moment later she touched down on the soft sand and skidded to a stop at

the water's edge. She hid the board in some bushes and started off to find the lab.

"Halt! Who goes there?"

Natasha froze.

Two men ran onto the beach. One of them was holding a leash, at the end of which was a snarling dog with many sharp teeth. The dog sniffed the air and then spun in her direction with a loud bark. The threesome moved toward her.

Natasha sprinted into the woods.

Nice doggy! Wish I had something to give you to keep you busy for a while—like five hundred pounds of hamburger!

As she ran, she scanned the area for a tall tree with thick limbs. If she could launch herself onto a sturdy branch, she might be able to elude the men.

At last she saw the perfect limb. She leaped and pressed the antigravitational button on her elbow pad, expecting the device to send her rocketing into the air.

Nothing happened.

Mind memo, item one: Recharge elbow pad when you get home!

Thinking fast, she unclipped a grappling hook from her utility belt and let out the line. She flung the hook over the branch, gave a sharp tug to secure it, and then pressed a button on her belt. The line retracted, pulling her high into the tree. She stowed the hook and flattened herself against the branch.

Your move, she thought.

Her pursuers crashed out of the shadows.

"Stupid pricker bush," one of the guards muttered.

"Quiet! Can't you see Fang is onto something?"

Fang made straight for her tree and sniffed it.

Uh-oh, Natasha thought.

Fang lifted his leg and peed on the trunk.

"Oh, that's nice," the first guard said with disgust. "Come on, let's get out of here."

"What about the intruder?"

"What intruder? Fang was probably chasing a squirrel."

"No squirrel makes that kind of noise!" the second guard argued.

"A buffalo, then. Didn't you say you saw one the other night?"

"I said I *thought* I saw one. It might have been a rock." The threesome moved away.

Natasha held still until she was sure they were gone. Then she adjusted her super-powered glasses and scanned the surrounding area in search of Lubek's lab.

Tree. Tree. Buffalo-shaped rock. Small furry animal. Shrub. Van. Tree—hold on!

She zeroed in on a cargo van lumbering along a bumpy dirt road.

Ten to one it's going to the lab!

She swung out of the tree and raced after the vehicle. The van was moving so slowly that she had no trouble catching up to it and hoisting herself onto its roof.

Five minutes later, the van bounced to a stop. Natasha sneaked a peek. They were outside a gate. Beyond the gate was a small building.

One lab, dead ahead!

The gate rumbled open and the van drove

inside.

Look out, Lubek, here I come!

Chapter Five

Lubek at the Controls

The van parked behind the lab. The driver unloaded a big box, locked up, and disappeared into the building.

Natasha crept down from the roof. Using the van as cover, she surveyed the building. She spotted an open window and tiptoed to it. Strange noises came from inside.

Brrzap! Blam! Blam! Zing! Wackawacka-wackawacka!

Natasha frowned. *I've heard those sounds*

before. . . .

She looked through the window. The lab was one big room. One wall was taken up by a giant video screen. Natasha blinked in surprise.

On the screen was the game KC had downloaded from the high school's Web site!

Just then, whoever was at the controls clicked to the game's main menu. Natasha couldn't see the person, so she studied the menu instead.

The game had several adventures from which to choose. One segment was an alien battle scene with lots of explosions and spaceships. Another featured souped-up race cars zooming around a track. In still another, players faced challenges, solved riddles, and found hidden objects. There was sports action, too, including football, basketball, and skateboarding.

A little something for everyone, she realized.

The controller selected a game. A three-legged alien on roller skates and a surfer dude on a pogo stick appeared. The controller pressed start and the figures took off in a race.

Then the alien and the dude froze.

"I'll put one here," the game player muttered. He turned his chair so he was facing the window. Natasha sucked in her breath.

Lubek!

Her uncle tapped the keys and the image on the screen changed once again. Now, instead of a roller-skating alien and a pogo-sticking dude, there were words. Natasha gulped when she read them: *Lubek is the best!*

I've heard that before, too! KC had said those exact words the night before— while he was playing the game!

"And now, replay!" Lubek punched some buttons.

The figures began the race. As they sped forward, lights flashed and blinked in the background and funny beeps, squawks, and howls sounded out of the speakers. But to Natasha's puzzlement, the Lubek message didn't reappear.

When the race ended—the alien won—Lubek spoke into a microphone. "Bring in the test subjects."

Test subjects?!

A small group of people entered the room.

"Please be seated," Lubek said in an oily voice.

When they were settled in a row of comfortable chairs, Lubek restarted the race sequence again. Once more, the alien and the dude tore across on the screen. Natasha watched along

with the "test subjects." Some of the people laughed at the crazy antics and a few of them took sides, cheering for one figure or the other.

"You enjoyed the game?" Lubek asked when the race was over.

The people murmured their agreement.

"Is the game something you would like to have?"

More murmurs and a few vigorous nods.

"Do any of you know the name of the person who created this game?"

This time the people shook their heads.

"His name is . . . *Lubek.*"

"I love Lubek!" a man shouted.

"Lubek is the *best*!" sang a woman.

"All hail Lubek!" came a third yell.

"Lubek can do no wrong!" cried a voice behind them.

The crowd went suddenly silent. Several people turned in their seats to the window where the cry had come from. But there was no one there.

"Who said that?" Lubek demanded.

Cowering beneath the window, Natasha pressed her fist into her mouth.

I did! she thought incredulously.

Chapter Six

Discovered!

It's that game.

Even as she thought it, Natasha knew she was right. Something about that game made people believe that Lubek was a wonderful person.

The sound of footsteps broke into Natasha's thoughts. Her shout had given away her presence. Lubek and his men were hunting for her!

She ran across the pavement and rolled under the cargo van.

Safe! she thought as Lubek's guards ran past.

Then a car door slammed, a motor started, and the van backed out, leaving  her lying in plain view on the driveway.

 She scrambled to her feet and followed the moving vehicle.

I'll swing in the open window feet first, kick the driver out, grab the steering wheel, crash through the gate, and race to safety! she thought, heart pounding with anticipation.

The van drove around the building and pulled into another parking spot. The driver got out, locked the door, and walked away whistling.

Okay, so I break a window, hot-wire the ignition, and roar through the gates to freedom!

She picked up a large rock. Then she paused.

The van was right next to the fence that surrounded the building.

I guess I could just jump the fence. Boring, but quieter. She dropped the rock and climbed back to the van's roof. She took a running start and—*gotta add a little pizzazz!*—somersaulted over the fence. She landed with a soft thud on the other side.

"Halt! Who goes there?"

Fang and his handlers crashed out of the under-brush.

Not again, she groaned, melting as quickly and

quietly as she could into the shadows.

Not quickly or quietly enough, unfortunately. A beam from a flashlight caught her just before she ducked behind a rock.

"Hey, there really *is* an intruder!" one of the guards said with surprise. "Think we should go after her?"

"'Think we should go after her?'" the other guard mimicked. "Duh! That's only our job!"

"No, our job is to patrol the beach!"

"Our job is to keep intruders off the island!"

"Right! By patrolling the beach!"

While the guards bickered, Natasha pulled her cell phone from her belt and dialed Oleg's number.

Something snuffled her ear.

Woof?

It was Fang. His canine face was full of amazement, as if he hadn't really expected to find anything.

"Natasha, did you just bark at me?" Oleg's

confused voice came from her cell.

"Oleg, thank goodness!" she whispered urgently.

Woof. Fang cocked his head as if pondering his next move.

Natasha, on the other hand, knew exactly what her next move should be—run, before the guards came to investigate!

She stood up and took a few steps away.

Woof! Fang lunged after her. *Woo—gluh!* The leash pulled taut, jerking Fang off his feet.

"What's *wrong* with that fool dog?" a new

and very angry voice demanded.

Natasha's blood turned cold. *Lubek!*

She took off into the woods. "Oleg, I'm on my way to the beach! Be there with the copter—and send down the rope ladder!"

There was a moment of silence. "Um, I can't do that," he said finally.

"Excuse me?!" Natasha took off at a dead run through the woods.

"Lubek's searchlight stayed on me after you dropped. I had to land the copter in the lake. But listen, you get to the beach and I'll pick you up! Don't worry!"

Natasha didn't have time to talk further.

Lubek, Fang, and the guards were closing in.
Don't worry, he says!

Chapter Seven

Natasha Loves Lubek?!

Natasha raced full speed through the under-brush toward the beach.

"*Oof!*"

She tripped over her airboard. Snatching it up, she hurried onto the beach and looked for Oleg.

He was nowhere to be seen.

Her pursuers, however, were in plain sight. "We've got you now, intruder!" one of the guards yelled.

Natasha dropped the airboard and assumed a fighting stance. "Not yet, you don't!"

"What should we do?" the guard asked Lubek.

"Get her!"

"Oh, okay!"

The guard rushed her. Natasha dropped to a crouch and stuck out a leg.

"Who-o-oa!" The guard fell face first in the sand.

Woof! Fang rushed to his side and licked him with frantic concern.

The second guard charged. Natasha grabbed his outstretched arms and flipped him off his feet. He landed on his back next to the first guard. Now Fang had two faces to slobber.

Natasha beckoned to Lubek. "Come and get me," she growled.

Lubek bared his teeth.

Suddenly, the helicopter—or watercopter, since it was riding on pontoons—roared in toward shore.

"Swim for it!" Oleg called.

"You'll have to get through us first!" Lubek shouted. "Form a wall, boys!"

The guards jumped to their feet and got in line behind Lubek.

"*Gahh! Beside* me, you idiots!"

As the guards shuffled into place, Natasha

glanced down at her airboard.

I wonder. . . . She strapped the board onto her feet.

Now I'll throw the grappling hook around the tail of the copter, yell for Oleg to step on it, burst through Lubek's "wall" on my airboard-slash-water ski, and zoom across the lake to safety!

This time, her dramatic escape plan actually worked.

This is awesome! she thought as she wove back and forth in the copter's wake.

The copter left the water and shot into the air.

Not so awesome anymore! She hurriedly

pressed the retract button on her belt. The line zipped her upward. Oleg held the copter in place while she swung into the open door and climbed inside.

"Give a girl a little warning next time," she grumbled to Oleg.

"Sorry." Oleg swung the copter toward the mainland. "Did you find out what Lubek is up to?"

"Lubek is the best!" Natasha clapped a hand over her mouth.

Oleg looked at her in alarm. "That was creepy."

She took her hand away. "Say that name again," she whispered.

"You mean Lubek?"

"All hail Lubek!"

Oleg grabbed her arm. "Natasha, what is going on?"

She explained every weird thing that had happened in the past day—her friends' curious behavior, the words she'd seen on the screen in Lubek's lab, and how she and the test subjects had somehow been brainwashed after viewing the game.

Oleg slowly nodded. "Subliminal messages."

"Sub—what?"

"Subliminal messages," he repeated. "Very short messages or images that can be hidden in television shows, commercials, music, and, I guess, video games. We don't realize that we've seen the messages—but our brains pick up on them. And then our brains tell us to act on what we've seen."

"I'm not sure I follow," Natasha said.

"Here's the classic example," Oleg said. "You're in the cinema watching a movie. A subliminal message—say, the image of buttery popcorn and the word 'hungry'—flashes in the midst of the action. It's only there for a microsecond, but suddenly, you're craving popcorn. And then—"

"—I head to the concession counter to buy some?"

Oleg nodded. "That's what the people who sell popcorn hope you'll do, anyway."

Natasha thought for a moment. "So if Lu—er, you-know-who hides messages about how great he is in this video game and kids download the game and play it over and over—"

"—they'll be exposed to his subliminal messages over and over. They will start thinking that Lu—er, you-know-who is great. And if the children of Zoravia start playing the game—"

"—they'll start thinking he should be king of Zoravia!" Natasha finished. "Oleg, we've got to find a way to destroy that game! And I know just the place to start. Come on!"

Chapter Eight

Hackers 'R' Us

Natasha and Oleg landed the copter, raced back to the O'Brien's house, and sneaked into Natasha's room.

"KC was playing the game earlier," Natasha said as she sat at her computer, "so unless he deleted it—doubtful, he never deletes anything except homework assignments—we should be able to access it."

She started clicking through the list of programs on her computer.

"Aha! Got it!" She pushed back from the desk, stood up, and waved a hand at the keyboard. "Your turn. You're better at hacking than I am."

Oleg cracked his knuckles like a concert pianist and sat down. His fingers flew over the keys. Pictures, numbers, and letters flashed across the screen as he dug deeper and deeper, trying to trace the game's point of origin.

"Lubek covered his tracks well," he muttered. He looked at Natasha with alarm. "Sorry!"

"What?" Then her eyes widened. "You said Lubek! And I didn't say anything weird!" She pumped her fist. "Yes! The subliminal messages are wearing off!"

"Probably because you only saw a few of them. If you were exposed to more over a longer period of time, the effect might still be with you," Oleg mused. He typed some additional commands then gave a cry of triumph. "Found it!"

Natasha looked over his shoulder. "Excellent! Can you destroy it?"

Oleg didn't answer.

"Well, can you?"

"I can," Oleg replied slowly, "but I'm not sure I should."

Natasha stared at him with surprise. Then

surprise gave way to understanding. "Lubek knows spies were on his island. If we destroy the game, he'll know we've figured out his plan."

"And," Oleg added, "he might trace the destruction back to this computer. Then he'd find you. That is unacceptable."

Natasha paced the room. "But we can't just leave the game there, ready to be downloaded by some unsuspecting student or Zoravian!"

"No," Oleg agreed.

Natasha stopped pacing. "What if we just tinker with it instead? Find all the messages and remove them but leave the game itself unchanged?"

Oleg looked thoughtful. "That will work to protect the children of Zoravia because it hasn't been launched for download there yet. But what about all the kids at school who have already downloaded the game? How will the game we change reach them?"

"Simple," Natasha replied. "Lubek was adding more messages when I was on the island, remember? I'll bet he's going to offer a free update on the school Web site. We'll just wait for that update and swap our cleaned-up version with his!"

Oleg nodded, stood up, and crossed to the window. "Okay. I'll go back to my place and get to work on removing the messages. If Lubek suspects anything, the anti-hacking programs on my computer should throw him off track. Meanwhile, you monitor the school's Web site on your computer. My guess is that Lubek

will post the update tonight rather than giving us more time to stop him. When he does, contact me and I'll make the swap. Sound good?"

"Sounds perfect!"

Chapter Nine

Night Moves

After seeing Oleg safely out the window, Natasha changed out of her spy suit and into her pajamas. She logged onto the school's  Web site and clicked on an icon marked FUN FOR STUDENTS! Another icon, this one for access to Lubek's game, popped up. She was tempted to click on it—after all, the game did look pretty darn fun—but decided it was too risky.

The last thing I need is to start spouting support for Lubek again! Instead, she checked to make sure there was no information about a new, free download. There wasn't. So she sat back and waited.

Time ticked by. One hour. Natasha picked up a novel from her bedside table and started reading.

Two hours. She finished the book and tossed it aside.

Two and a half. Natasha yawned and eyed her bed. Her warm, soft, comfortable bed.

Three hours. Natasha's lids drooped.

Three hours and five minutes. Natasha slumped over her keyboard and fell fast asleep.

Beep!

"I'm awake! I'm awake!" Natasha lurched up, the side of her face  looking like a waffle from the indentations made by the keys. She looked around, wondering what had woken her.

Beep!

 It was her computer. Next to the game icon was a flashing message: *Free update for the best game in town! Download now?*

Natasha flipped open her cell phone and dialed Oleg's number.

"Ha-oh?" a sleepy voice answered.

"Oleg, is that you?"

The person on the other end cleared his throat. "*Harrumph.* Yes, s'me. S'you, 'tasha?"

"Were you *asleep?*"

"Me?" Oleg gave a mighty yawn. "No!"

"Yeah, right," Natasha said sarcastically. "Me either. Listen, the update is there. Finally. Were you able to remove all the messages?"

"Done," Oleg replied, sounding more awake. "But let's test it. Say his name."

"You mean Lubek?"

"Yes." Oleg was quiet

for a moment then gave a satisfied laugh. "Nothing! I played the game for two hours before going to—er, that is, before playing it for another hour. If I had failed to remove all the messages, I'm sure I would be telling you how wonderful I think Lubek is."

"Great work, Oleg. Can you make the swap?"

She heard him crack his knuckles again. "I'm on it."

"Do you need me for anything else tonight?"

"No," Oleg replied.

"Good." She stood up and stretched. "I'm a little worn out from all that airboarding, running through the woods, and water skiing."

"I hear you," Oleg said sympathetically. "All this typing has me worn out, too."

"I'm going to contact my dad and then head to bed." She pulled out her Booferberry. "And thanks again, Oleg. You're the best."

"Good night, Princess."

"See you at school on Monday. Have a good weekend."

Chapter Ten

Everybody Loves Natasha—and Oleg?!

After she informed her father of their success, Natasha slept like a log for the three remaining hours of the night. Saturday and Sunday passed in a blur of homework, housework, and mealtimes with the O'Briens.

When Monday morning came, she had to drag herself out of bed when her alarm clock sounded.

Shower, she thought blearily, *must . . . get . . . hot . . . shower!*

She threw on an old bathrobe and bumbled into the hallway, eyes at half-mast and hair sticking up like the business end of a broom. She glanced in the hall mirror and started.

Yee-ikes. Somebody find me a rock to crawl under, quick!

As she passed Greg's bedroom on the way to the bathroom, she heard familiar sounds.

Brrzap! Blam! Blam! Zing! Wackawackawackawacka!

He's playing Lubek's game, she realized. *Sure hope it's the one Oleg changed.*

Just then the sounds stopped and Greg's door opened.

Natasha prayed for the floor to swallow her whole before Greg saw her.

Please, she implored silently, *I don't have the*

strength to trade insults with him right now!

"Natasha!" Greg cried. "You look *awesome* this morning!"

She rolled her eyes. "Ha-ha, very funny. I know I look like the dog's dinner, thank you

very much!" She tried to push by him into the bathroom.

Greg laughed loud and long. "You have the greatest sense of humor!"

Natasha slammed the door in his face. She put the shower on as hot as she could stand it and stood under the spray for fifteen minutes. When she was done she felt mostly human again.

She threw on her robe and opened the bathroom door, ready to face the day.

Instead she found herself facing Greg.

"*Aau-u-ugh*! Why are you standing there?!"

"Wanna ride to school today?" he asked eagerly.

She was taken aback by his enthusiasm— and his question. He had never offered her a ride before. "Uh, sure. Um, can I get dressed first?"

"Why bother? You look great just like that!"

Natasha looked down at her thick terry cloth robe. "Ri—igh—t," she said slowly. "Well, I'll see you downstairs."

"Okay, great! That'll give me time to play a few more rounds of that game from the school Web site. Have you played it at all? I've been playing it all weekend. So has everyone else I know!" He disappeared into his room. Natasha heard *brrzaps* and *zings* coming from behind his door again.

Ten minutes later, she and Greg were on their way to school. At least the boy beside her *looked* like Greg. But he sure didn't *act* like Greg. Greg never listened to anything she said. This boy hung on her every word and tossed her compliments the way an old man tosses bread crumbs to a duck. By the end of the ride, she was thoroughly wigged out by his strange behavior.

I can't believe I ever wanted him to pay more attention to me, she thought as she escaped into the girl's bathroom. When she dared to leave a few minutes later, she was relieved to see he had gone.

But her relief vanished a moment later when she overheard something even stranger than Greg's compliments.

"Oleg, will you sit with me at lunch today?"

"No fair! He promised to sit with me, didn't you?"

She spun and saw an unusual sight. Oleg Boynski, school misfit, was proudly marching down the hall, flanked by two girls and followed by a stream of others, all of whom seemed to worship the ground he walked on!

Oleg broke free from his fans when he saw her. "Good morning, Natasha!"

"Natasha?!" The crowd of students

gasped as one. "Natasha is the best!"

"Natasha is the—?"

She narrowed her eyes at Oleg, suddenly suspicious.

"Come with me," she growled. She grabbed his arm and dragged him into an empty class-room. "Oleg, something tells me you didn't

stop tinkering with Lubek's game after you removed his messages. Something tells me you added *new* messages about how wonder-ful I am and how great you are!"

He gave her a mischievous look.

"Well, fine, enjoy it for today," she said,

throwing up her hands. "But take them out tonight, please! Because if you don't"—she drew a finger across her throat—"it's game over, pal!"